MATTHEW AND THE
MIDNIGHT
BANK

Published in Canada in 2000 by
Stoddart Kids,
a division of Stoddart Publishing Co. Limited
34 Lesmill Road
Toronto, ON M3B 2T6
Tel (416) 445-3333 Fax (416) 445-5967
E-mail cservice@genpub.com

Published in the United States in 2001 by
Stoddart Kids,
a division of Stoddart Publishing Co. Limited
180 Varick Street, 9th Floor
New York, New York 10014
Toll free 1-800-805-1083
E-mail gdsinc@genpub.com

Distributed in Canada by
General Distribution Services
325 Humber College Blvd.,
Toronto, ON M9W 7C3
Tel (416) 213-1919 Fax (416) 213-1917
E-mail cservice@genpub.com

Distributed in the United States by
General Distribution Services
4500 Witmer Industrial Estates, PMB 128
Niagara Falls, New York 14305-1386
Toll free 1-800-805-1083
E-mail gdsinc@genpub.com

Canadian Cataloguing in Publication Data

Morgan, Allen, 1946–
Matthew and the midnight bank

ISBN 0-7737-6134-9

I. Martchenko, Michael. II. Title.

PS8576.O642M263 2000   jC813'.54   C00-931096-7
PZ7.M67Mat 2000

Matthew's daytime Monopoly game and his worries
about money set the stage for a zany midnight bank adventure
involving money trees, robbers, and dreams of being rich.

We acknowledge for the financial support of our publishing program
the Government of Canada through the Book Publishing Industry Development Program (BPIDP),
the Canada Council, and the Ontario Arts Council.

Printed and bound in Hong Kong, China
by Book Art Inc., Toronto

MATTHEW AND THE
MIDNIGHT
BANK

by Allen Morgan
Illustrated by Michael Martchenko

Stoddart
Kids

TORONTO • NEW YORK

One day when it was rainy outside, Matthew decided to stay indoors and play a game of Secret Monopoly. He covered the table with blankets and sheets, then he set up the board on the floor underneath.

"You'll like this game a lot," Matthew told his mother. "You play it the same as the regular way, except for the flashlights and masks. Some of the rules are different as well. I'll tell them to you as we go along."

"I'm afraid I can't play right now," said his mother. "I have to balance my checkbook and pay the bills."

Matthew could see that she was really busy, so he rolled the dice and made all her moves for her. She did pretty well, at least for a while. Then she landed on all of Matthew's properties. Matthew grinned as he opened his money bag.

"You're losing all your money, Mom," he called up cheerfully.

"It certainly looks that way," she sighed as she eyed the pile of bills.

A little while later the rain stopped falling. Matthew tied his money bag to his belt and went outside. He found a penny by the front porch steps. He was about to go in and give it to his mother when he looked through the window. She seemed pretty sad as she worked on her checkbook. Matthew decided she'd need more than a penny, so he dug a hole underneath a bush and planted it there.

"Maybe it'll grow and make us rich," Matthew thought, as he patted the dirt into place. Then he went up onto the front porch and rang the wind chimes for luck.

Later that night when it was time for bed, Matthew checked his money bag. He'd done pretty well at Monopoly, but still, even so, he felt a bit worried.

"Are we going to run out of money?" he asked, as his mother tucked him in.

"No, we're not," she assured him. "We still have plenty left."

"Where is it all?"

"It's in the bank. They'll keep it safe and help it to grow so we'll have even more when we need it." She kissed him goodnight and turned out the light.

"I wish I could help our money grow, too," Matthew thought as he closed his eyes. Just before he fell asleep, he heard the sound of the wind chimes outside ringing softly in the night.

Around about midnight Matthew woke up. The moon was bright and the wind was blowing. The jingling sound of the chimes filled the air — they seemed to be ringing everywhere! Matthew went to the window to see what was happening. The bush below was all aglow. Small shining pouches were growing from the branches. One popped open as Matthew watched and sparkling coins tumbled out.

Matthew grabbed his money bag and ran outside. There were lots of coins on the ground under the bush. When Matthew finished picking them up, his bag was completely full.

Just then, a man on a scooter came down the street. He noticed Matthew and stopped at the curb.

"Looks like you're rolling in dough tonight, the same as me!" he said with a grin. "Fargo's the name, makin' money's my game."

"My name is Matthew. My game is mostly Monopoly."

"Great blazing billionaires, that's excellent news! I've been looking all night for a guy like you! They're having a Midnight Monopoly game at the bank tonight. All the best players are going to be there. It's bigger than Bingo and safer than Sorry — or so they say. You gotta play with a partner though. You want to team up?"

When Matthew agreed to give it a try, Fargo beamed and stuck out his hand. "We'll split the winnings right down the middle," he said, as they shook on the deal. "Fifty-fifty at least. Sixty-sixty or more, one hundred percent for sure!"

When they arrived at the midnight bank, there were lots of trucks lined up outside. Matthew watched as they unloaded their coins down a big metal chute that went through the pavement and into the basement below.

There were rows and rows of bank machines beside the front door. Some played music, others paid cash, a few spewed confetti and one made rude noises. Most of the customers waiting in line looked a little confused.

"Good thing we have lots of money already," said Fargo. "We can just pass Go and move right along."

Inside the midnight bank, the game was about to begin.

"You know what to do," Fargo told Matthew. "Just buy and sell and roll your dice, make lots of money and try to be nice — when you can. The game won't end until someone lands on the Free Barking square. That's lots of fun. Everyone barks and runs around while they count all the cash to see which team won."

"Are there any special rules I should know?"

"Lots," Fargo said. "But mainly the game runs by rule number one. It's not written down, but everyone knows what it says."

As it turned out, rule number one really covered a lot. The players rolled their dice whenever they wanted and no one took turns. Everyone had different money to spend. Beavers had cedar chips, bulls used bells. The bears traded foil-wrapped chocolate coins, while the penguins had coupons and the loons used balloons. A few confused ducks tried to make a fast buck with a box of old greenbacks.

All of a sudden a big bell rang and everyone shouted, "It's Bonus Time!" They threw their money up into the air and grabbed what they could as it fell down again.

Not far from Matthew, some dangerous pigeons stood waiting and watching the scene. As everyone dashed for the cascading cash, they opened a trap door and snuck down inside. They looked quite suspicious, so Matthew followed through the trap door, too.

The stairs led down to the basement below. It was pretty dark except for the glow from a massive furnace. Matthew put on his Secret Monopoly mask and flicked on his flashlight. A stream of coins slid down the chute from the street above. A groundhog sorted them into piles. A mole scooped pennies into wheelbarrows, then tossed all the rest in the furnace. A crew of raccoons rolled the pennies away. The dangerous pigeons grabbed a wheelbarrow and joined the line of raccoons. Matthew decided to do the same.

"Don't give me away," he whispered to the mole. "I'm in disguise."

"That's what you raccoons always say," said the mole. "Move along now. We're about to make our new mega-coins and we don't want to mix in those pennies."

"Why are the coins so big?" Matthew wanted to know.

"Gotta keep up with inflation, you know. A nickel won't buy many pickles these days, and a quarter's not worth a dime."

The raccoons rolled their pennies up a long wooden ramp, and came out in the bank's central courtyard. Money trees grew everywhere. Their leaves were rustling in the breeze. Matthew hid behind one and watched secretly. The raccoons dumped out their pennies and dug them into the ground all around the trees. The dangerous pigeons followed their lead, but when the raccoons went back down for more, the pigeons stayed behind. They picked the leaves from the money trees and tucked them under their wings. Matthew had seen enough.

"You're robbing the bank! You should go directly to jail!" he cried as he stepped out of hiding.

Alarm bells went off. A siren wailed. Searchlights snapped on and the robbers were nailed.

A security helicopter swooped overhead and scooped all the pigeons up into a net.

"Excellent work!" the pilot called down. "You've saved the bank a whole lot of dollars. You'll get a reward for sure."

Matthew was pleased, but he had to get back in the game. Fargo was holding his own all alone and he might need some help from his partner. So the pilot gave Matthew a lift in his chopper and lowered him back onto the board through one of the skylights. He landed right on the Free Barking Square. This ended the game and all the players started to howl. They yipped and woofed and barked and growled. The din was simply amazing.

Fargo rushed over and shook Matthew's hand. His grin stretched from ear to ear.

"Well played, partner, we're bound to win! I've got lots of money, I bet you do, too!"

Matthew opened his money bag to show what he had. It wasn't exactly what Fargo had hoped. In fact, it was nothing at all.

"I threw all my money into the air," Matthew explained. "Then something happened and I didn't have time to get any back."

Before he could tell Fargo more, a raccoon appeared with a big burlap sack.

"Here's your reward for catching those pigeons," he told Matthew.

"Holy jumping jelly rolls!" Fargo exclaimed when he saw what it was. "That's one of the bank's new mega-coins!"

The mega-coin was worth quite a lot. When all their money was finally counted, Matthew and Fargo had won hands down. They divided it up and shared it all out. Matthew stuffed his money into his bag and dragged it to the deposit window.

"I'd like to balance my mother's account," he said as he plunked it down on the counter.

The teller brought out the banking scales and put a huge checkbook on one of the trays. Then she poured Matthew's winnings out onto the other. When the trays were finally even, she gave him a paper marked Paid in Full. There was even some money left over.

"I guess I'll take the rest home in cash," Matthew decided.

Fargo agreed that was what he should do, then he drove Matthew home on his scooter. "You're the very best partner I've ever had. Come out some night and play again," he called as he drove away.

"Okay," Matthew said, as he waved goodbye. Then he went inside and climbed into bed. Soon he was fast asleep.

Around about six Matthew woke up. He ran right away to his mother's room to tell her the good news.

"We're rich! We're rich!" Matthew announced as he bounced on the bed. Then he threw all his money up into the air so his mother could see what they had.

"We're what?" asked his mother, as she opened one eye.

"Rich!" Matthew cried. "Well, at least I am, and you're my best mom, so I'll let you keep whatever you want — except for the hundred or so we'll want for some candy and gum."

His mother didn't quite understand, so Matthew explained about the Midnight Monopoly he'd played at the bank. She still seemed confused, so he gave her the paper marked Paid in Full and made her get out of bed.

"You can be rich just the same as me," Matthew said, as he led her outside. "But first, you'll need a money bush to get you started."

"What I need right now to get me started is a cup of coffee," his mother insisted.

Matthew knew his mother well. Once she got hold of her mug of brew there was no way of telling just what she might do, so he made her choose her money bush first.

"I'll tell you everything at breakfast, Mom," he said, as he gave her a penny to plant.

"While we're eating, you can practice barking. And then when you're done, I'll teach you all about rule number one."